THE CHRONICLES OF DINAH LEE WRIGHT VOLUME 2

TALES OF AN OLD WEST SORCERESS

STEPHANNIE TALLENT

For more information, contact: stephannie@stephannietallent.com

First e-Book edition May 2021

eBook ISBN: 978-1-942655-20-6
Print ISBN: 978-1-942655-19-0

www.stephannietallent.com

To Dave

The desert wears... a veil of mystery. Motionless and silent it evokes in us an elusive hint of something unknown, unknowable, about to be revealed. Since the desert does not act it seems to be waiting — but waiting for what?

— EDWARD ABBEY

CONTENTS

INTRODUCTION

Included herein are the additional tales of Dinah, a traveling sorceress in an alternate Old West, where magic is used by the bold, and both monsters and gods reside.

THE FOX SORCERER

Dinah blinked.

The Chinese man was still there, strolling down the muddy, wheel-rutted Main Street of West Jordan, jewel-encrusted crimson silk robe glittering in the hot early afternoon August sun.

Steam from the mud puddles licked around the Chinese man's cream leather boots and the hem of his robe, but not a spot of mud dared to mar either boots or robe.

The sleeves of his robe draped over his hands, but Dinah bet his hands were soft and his nails manicured. His long narrow queue danced around his shoulders like a string to a kite being tossed by a breeze. That same soft wind blew the scents of sage, mint, and chrysanthemum tea towards her.

His cheekbones were sharp as knives, his black eyes glinting and prideful. He looked like a prince in the prime of life, something out of a fairy tale Dinah's mama had told her when Dinah was just a child. When Dinah was content and safe and loved, with her mama and papa. 'Stead of always on edge, wondering if she could earn enough for a meal after paying for her mule Malyu's feed.

Two uncanny sandy-colored foxes gamboled behind the Chinese

man, their pale paws as pristine as his boots. Spirit foxes, in material form. One glanced at her, tongue lolling in a vulpine smirk, white teeth gleaming, as it—he—bounced along. The smaller fox yipped and barked, amber eyes flashing as she glanced at Dinah.

No one else reacted. 'Course, there weren't many people out in the late summer monsoon mugginess.

The next block over, the young black hostler, Jimmy, led a fine little black-and-white paint mare to the livery behind the town's single boarding house. That little mare would join Malyu, tucked away with fresh hay.

Dinah liked Jimmy. He'd slipped Malyu a treat of sweet oats the night before, and laid out fresh hay for Dinah to sleep on.

Closer to, Mrs McKinney, pale pretty face pinched and dour in the shade of her bonnet, left the two-story general store with a basket of apples and a small roll of lace ribbon, gingham skirts swishing along.

And heading right towards Dinah and the Chinese man, Deputy Batson strolled down the street to the adobe building that served as his office and jail, touching his fingers to his felted wool fedora as he passed Mrs. McKinney. Mrs. McKinney nodded to him, but her eyes skated right past Dinah's when she walked by Dinah. To her, Dinah was lower than the fat ruby-carapaced dung beetles rolling around in the street near the horse droppings, and not near as pretty.

'Course Deputy Batson didn't bother tipping his hat to Dinah, neither. He tolerated her, but that was it.

Not a one even seemed to see the Chinese man and his foxes.

Dinah trusted her instincts. And her instincts were screaming that if no one else saw this man strolling down the center of Main Street, brazen as a snake oil salesman, like he owned every last building and every single person in town, she ought to pretend she couldn't see him either. She knew, better than most, the prejudice against Chinese, being herself the daughter of a Chinese prostitute.

But she doubted someone so proud and aristocratic would hide his presence, unless he had a nefarious purpose.

She could discover that purpose later. Right now, she slunk back into the narrow shaded passageway between the saloon and boarding house, ignoring the pungent stink of piss. Luckily, she dressed like a boy: blunt toed leather boots, heavy canvas pants, and a loose-fitting shirt with a wool vest to hide her slim figure. No long skirts to drag in the muck.

Her long glossy hair was tied up in a loose bun off her neck, tucked up under a black wool felt hat. Sweat traced a warm wet trail down her spine.

Dinah hoped the Chinese sorcerer (for what else could he be, with those two fox spirits?) didn't catch a taste of her own small, lonely magics on the breeze.

She bit at a hangnail, drawing a rusty-tasting drop of blood that she smeared on the silver *Look-Away* charm she wore on a leather lace around her neck.

It seemed to work. Leastwise no fox or sorcerer turned down the passageway to confront her. Rather, they continued right on down the street, those foxes yapping as they pounced after grasshoppers coming to take sips of the rain puddles.

Dinah reckoned herself a cautious woman. As a bounty hunting, problem-solving, half-Chinese sorceress for hire, driven by her need for justice in a land that served little, aided by her own magics inherited from her mama, she had to be cunning and prudent and wary.

Not someone who'd let curiosity gnaw at her belly til she left that passageway to follow the sorcerer.

But that's what Dinah did.

THE CHINESE SORCERER set up camp a couple miles out of the far side of town, in the clearing under the desert willow trees that encircled the spring feeding Scott's Creek, the source of West Jordan's sweet water supply. Thick chaparral, snowberry, and juniper grew intermixed with the trees on either side of the trail leading up to the spring.

Dinah didn't take the trail.

She circled 'round to the far side of the spring, then laid down and crawled on her belly through the needle grass, under and around the scrub and rocks, til she found a suitable spot tucked behind a dreamy willow. She could see the sorcerer and still be downwind from those foxes. Aromatic creosote, piney and lemony, flavored the muggy air. She hoped it would help cover the stench of her sweat.

One fox lounged on a plush red rug in front of a small cream-colored silk tent. The tent was four feet tall, just big enough to give shelter to a thick pile of embroidered blankets and silk pillows.

The other fox lapped water from the clear spring, then dabbed a paw in, likely trying for a trout or crawdad.

The sorcerer tended a small ornate brass brazier, feeding it dried sticks and herbs. His over-robe hung from a branch, leaving him in heavy draping silk trousers and a woven linen shirt, the latter sheer in the leaf-dappled sunlight, showing off a mighty fine torso.

A wisp of sage-scented smoke wafted towards Dinah's hiding place, tickling her nose and watering her eyes. She kept staring, though, til she sneezed. Couldn't help herself.

The sneezing or the staring.

He didn't even look up, just kept feeding the brazier. "You might as well come over here," he said, his voice smooth as his silk trousers that outlined everything. Everything.

Dinah wasn't the sort to be distracted by matters of the flesh. No, she was not. No matter how pretty that flesh was. No matter how lonely she was.

The sorcerer smiled, a soft quirk of his upper lip, and added more herbs. Mint joined the sage, and Dinah parted her lips with the thought of how the sorcerer must taste, bright and fresh and sweet, those finely shaped lips of his against hers.

She knew some folks who were obsessed with earthly pleasures. Men who'd gambled away their ranches and cattle to try to win the attention of a woman, women who'd left their families to be in the arms of a scoundrel. She'd never understood it before. She'd seen the physical scars her mama bore, from before meeting Dinah's father, from clients savage with lust, and recognized the emotional scars that only her papa had healed.

Dinah didn't trust the idea of physical passion, and she was glad she herself had never desired anyone before. She was alone. By choice.

But now, a pulsing ached between her legs, a desperate need to go over to him, run her hands against that heavy silk of his trousers, even smooth her hands up under that linen shirt, stroking that muscled belly.

The sorcerer sprinkled fragments of dried yellow petals over the brazier. The scent of tea, invigorating and sharp, made her whole body tingle like it never had before.

The fox on the rug yipped and rolled over, waving those cute little dipped-in-cream paws in the air, brown eyes bright.

The fox that had been drinking from the spring shook itself off and trotted to the sorcerer, weaving around and between his legs like a big friendly tom cat.

Jealousy stabbed her. Why should that creature touch him, and not her?

"Come, do not fight it," cajoled the sorcerer.

And Dinah couldn't. Couldn't resist. Didn't even want to, anymore. She rose to her knees.

Mrs. McKinney appeared from behind one of the desert willows next to the trail, opposite to Dinah's hiding spot. Her blue gingham skirt was all stained with leaves and trail muck.

She walked right up to the sorcerer and sank into his arms with a sigh that turned to a deep throated moan, rubbing herself against him like a barn cat in heat.

Dinah gaped, her mind suddenly sharp, an icy chill running through her core.

She fumbled in her bag of charms hanging from her belt, finding the brass-plated mountain lion tooth charm. A charm for protection. She grabbed her knife out of its scabbard next to the charm bag and sliced the meat at the base of her left thumb, coating the charm with her blood, turning that brass into a stormfront sunset.

Dinah hoped the charm would be powerful enough.

The sorcerer quirked a fine eyebrow at Dinah's hiding place as he lowered his lips to Mrs. McKinney's and wrapped his lean muscled arms around her.

He kissed Mrs. McKinney hard, not even letting up for a breath until Mrs. McKinney swooned, then kept kissing her, til her face sunk in and her skin dried up and flaked away, til he was holding nothing but what looked like a rat caught up somewhere it couldn't get out, and it was three months later, all papery skin and brittle bones.

The little foxes danced around the two of them all the while, yipping and waving their bushy tails around as he sucked the life force out of Mrs. McKinney.

The sorcerer dropped what was left of Mrs. McKinney and stretched his arms to the sky in satisfaction. His heavy trousers were damp in the front.

Dinah figured he'd had a mighty good time, killing Mrs. McKinney.

Dinah wasn't ignorant. Just usually uninterested.

"Come out, come out," the sorcerer crooned, his voice trying to sneak through the charm's protections.

"I don't want any of what you're offering," Dinah called back. Nonetheless, she left her place behind the willow tree and stopped a few yards away from the sorcerer. She kept that brazier of his, still smoking tea and mint and sage, between the two of them.

She glanced at what remained of Mrs. McKinney. The larger fox, the male, was pawing at her gingham dress and shredding off bits of blue-checked fabric, tossing them in the air, batting at them. That seemed to bore him after a few moments, and he started digging and tearing through a sleeve til he got an arm bone. He settled down and began gnawing on it. It cracked like a gunshot when the fox broke it in two.

The other fox, the littler one, sat by the sorcerer's side, her amber eyes glinting in sly foxy amusement.

"What about," the sorcerer said, "the power to control the storms?" A shadow dashed over the clearing.

Dinah looked up straight overhead. Sure enough, monsoon storm clouds were roiling in, thunderheads heavy and dark with the devastating potential to cause floods and wildfires. Lightning itched at her palms, longing to be set free.

Her lion's-tooth charm flared, a spot of grounding heat against her left palm.

"The power to make those townspeople respect you, despite your birth. Despite the foreign cast to your features."

The charm burned hotter.

"Do you know what she was thinking, your Mrs. McKinney? What she feared?" he said softly. "Her foremost thought was not that she was dying. Rather, she couldn't face herself being willingly despoiled by a Chinaman.

"That's what they think of you, even when they hire you to hunt down their missing cattle, or discover who is cheating them, or whatever of the dozens of menial tasks they have you do. That you're nothing but occasionally useful trash."

Power. Power to never fear anyone again, power to give herself a life of luxury, power to be safe. Power to force folks to meet her eyes as an equal, not some bit of filth.

People killed each other for power.

Dinah didn't like to kill. She certainly did not like other folks trying to kill her.

She shook her head. "I don't want them to fear me, and that's all you're truly offering."

And she'd never, ever be safe. Always on guard, til someone managed to slit her throat out of fear or covetousness.

The charm cooled in her hand.

The storm clouds scudded away, taking away the lightning that wanted to nestle inside her.

The sorcerer gazed at Dinah, eyes narrowing, calculating. He quirked an eyebrow, kneeled to pat the little fox's head, then stood.

"So. Neither lust, nor power, is enough for you. Huli Fang," he said "go to her."

The little fox Huli Fang trotted over to Dinah and raised one creamy paw up to her.

"You are lonely," the sorcerer said. "I offer you Huli Fang. She will be your lifelong companion, always loving you, never leaving you. Your most trusted confident, the other half of your heart."

The charm burned so hot Dinah dropped it.

It exploded before it hit the ground, fragments of molten brass and ivory tooth flashing like stars. Some brass splattered on her left hand, scorching it, and she wiped her hand against her trousers furiously, tears streaming down her cheeks.

A chasm of loneliness, deep and lost, lay open and uncovered in her heart. Dinah knew it was truly there. All her life, since her mama and papa died, she'd been covering that hole with learning and travelling and work. Always alone, not fitting in with her papa's fancy people back East, who were aghast he'd settled with a Chinese woman. Never fitting in with the Chinese here, her mama a prostitute, lowest of the low.

That oubliette of misery and loneliness had grown deeper and deeper over the years, like an abandoned mine shaft being eaten away by an underground river.

Didn't matter that the charm was destroyed. It never could protect against this.

Dinah stroked Huli Fang's soft head. Like silk, her fur was. The fox licked her burnt hand, cooling it.

Dinah took one step, two, three towards the sorcerer. Mint and tea and sage swirled around her. Huli Fang walked with her, pressing her warm furry body close against Dinah's leg.

His handsome face relaxed, and she held out her burnt left hand to him. He took it, drawing her to him. His warm touch soothed the burns on her hand. His black eyes, amused and intrigued, met hers.

He smiled at her, and Dinah smiled right back.

She stabbed him in the heart with the knife held in her right hand. Aimed between his ribs, slipping in like a freshwater eel amongst the marsh grass.

He pushed her away, stumbling against the brazier, knocking it over, scattering the remaining bits of herbs and leaves. Dark crimson heart's blood drenched that fine linen shirt of his, molding it to his torso. The storm clouds rushed across the sky, and lightning struck a desert willow across the spring. Torrential rain doused any burning bits left over from the brazier.

Hail stones the size of peas pelted Dinah, the bite of each icy stone bringing her back to herself.

He fell, gasping, a bewildered look in his eyes. It didn't take long for him to die, those black pupils dilating, the wide deep darkness echoing the chasm in her heart. His handsome face, so smooth and pretty, dried up til he looked like what was left of Mrs. McKinney: a husk devoid of any remnant of life.

The hail stopped and the rain petered out.

The foxes, Huli Fang and her mate, their fur matted and soaked, stood stock still, gaping at her, jaws loose.

"Git," she said, dry-eyed, mopping rain from her brow. "I don't want you anyways."

DINAH HIKED BACK TO TOWN, carrying a makeshift bundle made of the sorcerer's tent, filled with his charms and other sorcerous paraphernalia. She'd study it all later, when she reached a safe spot away from West Jordan.

Dinah couldn't stay in West Jordan. She needed to pack up her mule, Malyu, and leave. Mrs. McKinney was going to be missed, if she wasn't already, and who better to blame than the half Chinese girl who tried to pass as a boy, and studied and used dark magics to boot?

Dinah didn't relish the thought of a noose around her neck. She'd seen that happen to enough people she knew were innocent, but whose foreign features or dark skin condemned them despite any inconvenient truths.

The foxes had run away after she rejected them. She couldn't forget seeing the male fox chewing on Mrs. McKinney's arm bone, sucking out the last bits of marrow. If they had minds enough to choose her, Dinah, (and that's the only way she'd have one as a companion), they had minds enough to have chosen the sorcerer and partaken in his wickedness.

That she couldn't abide.

She sorrowed for Mrs. McKinney, that sad weak woman, even though Mrs. McKinney wouldn't have thought twice about her. Or once, for that matter.

Sorrowed even more for the heady crazy rush of riding the storm clouds blowing across the sky, lightning in her hands.

Sorrowed about that chasm of loneliness, plunging deep into her heart, unfilled.

But she wasn't sorry for herself.

THE MONSOON

Dinah reined in her mule, Malyu, and stared down into the small rocky ravine. Sweat dripped down her neck, despite her pinning her long black hair up under her felt cowboy hat. She swiped at her face with a faded turkey-red bandanna, streaking it with sweat and trail dust.

Red-fruited prickly pear and fuzzy cholla cactus, glowing with the gold light of the setting sun, dotted the sides of the ravine.

Prickly pear with its stabby needles that drank down a China girl's blood as thirstily as anyone else's if you even thought to grab a fruit. Which she had. Once. Bland and watery, it hadn't been worth the bloodletting.

Even worse, cholla, with its loose stubby branches covered by fuzz. Those branches would break off if you came within jumping range. And that cotton fluff? Vicious fine needles, that you couldn't even see to pull out. They'd fester, sure enough. She'd run into one the week prior. Itched like the devil, but she couldn't pluck out the needles like regular honest splinters, so they just sat in her hand til her body dealt with them, oozing fluid and painfully puffy in the meantime.

A few saguaros tried vainly to hang on as well amidst their

shorter cousins, the shadows of their long arms clutching the canyon walls, their drooping demeanor betraying they knew they belonged elsewhere, up dancing on the rolling hills, not down here in this jagged little cut in the earth.

She actually liked the saguaros, of all the cacti. Elegant, with their reaching arms. She'd seen little tan striped owls nesting in holes in the trunks. Cute as a button. Saw a bobcat perched atop of one once too, all lazy with its big paws dangling, yellow eyes half lidded.

She just hoped a saguaro wouldn't lose its footing and come crashing down on her head. As Malyu picked her way down the narrow trail, avoiding the cacti, Dinah noted the skeleton of a broken-off saguaro near the creek, tan ribs casting a sad jagged shadow as the last rays of the sun poked into the canyon.

The stream at the bottom was just a trickle, smelling of wet limestone and dust, feeding into the Rillito River further west, which itself fed into the Santa Cruz River, running down into the grass and cottonwood filled valley that included the settlement of Tucson, an oasis in the desert.

Sure-footed Malyu could ford the Rillito no problem. Long as a flash flood didn't come crashing down between the cliffs.

A year ago Dinah and Malyu had been caught up in a flash flood in the slot canyons of Deseret Territory. She did not care to experience one again. Even a sorceress such as herself didn't lightly face the raw elements.

And it *was* monsoon season. Flash floods and fire on the mountain tops and everlasting lightning.

She saw the flare of far-off lightning illuminating the roof of the sky, smelled its sharpness, and heard the chasing crash of thunder.

Thankfully, the surrounding air remained dry.

Just so many things had gone wrong on her last job. Maybe her luck had changed.

Malyu barely got her hooves damp in the creek, iron shoes tinkling against the granite and limestone rocks washed down from the many colored stripes banding the mountains.

With Dinah's luck, Malyu would throw a shoe.

Malyu clambered up the other side, her thin tail swishing away biting flies attracted to her pungent mulish sweat. Dinah, leaning forward in the saddle to help Malyu climb, didn't fare so well: one tenacious critter grew fat off her blood, and even slow and drunk it easily avoided her half-hearted swats.

Up the other side, Dinah gazed at the Rincons. Thick heavy thunderheads rushed along the peaks. The sun had just dipped below the horizon, but the sky was a riot of deep scarlet and violet to the west, and deep indigo twilight punctuated by stabs of brilliant blue lightning to the east.

She'd never seen so much lightning in her life.

Or so many thunderbirds.

Dozens soared amongst the thunderheads, spinning and plummeting only to rise with heavy beats of raincloud colored wings. They didn't avoid the lightning. Either they drew the lightning, or they sought it out. Forks of lightning zapped the thunderbirds every other strike, limning their huge raptor bodies with glowing azure. She could see sparks flying off the tips of their wing feathers like shooting stars.

If she could fly like that, she wouldn't even care about the vexations of the past few weeks.

Big fat warm rain drops thwopped against her tan buffalo felt hat, a gift from the rancher she'd helped out in Mesa Verde. He'd felt sorry for her. Oh, she'd solved his problem, an infestation of Ixhunpedzkins, tiny relatives of the indigenous Gila lizards, those peach- and black-speckled, slow-moving, mild-mannered lizards.

Gilas were venomous, yes, but you had to poke one to get it annoyed, then open its mouth for it, then stick your hand in, for it to even bother to bite you.

The Ix-hunpedzkins, brilliantly beaded beasts of obsidian and coral, with biting front ends and stinging back ends, and foul tempers to boot, could incapacitate an entire working ranch in just a day. They'd bite a person or sting them, just out of meanness. The worst would bite a person's shadow, sneaky-like, causing a splitting headache that could rupture vessels in the victim's brain, without them even knowing they were attacked.

She'd lost most of her amulets in the process of clearing out the Ix-hunpedzkins, as well as her old battered wool hat. That, too, was when she had tangled with a cholla cactus, while hunting down the very last of the miniscule beady eyed lizards.

The small bag of coins the rancher paid her wouldn't go far to replace the amulets. She could hex a handful on her own given time and materials, but others were, frankly, beyond her current skills. The important ones. *Healing, Protection, Guarding.*

Least-wise she still had her *Look-Away* charm.

As well as the buffalo felt hat, he'd given her a lead for a job, at a bordello in Tucson, apparently run over with other sorts of magical vermin.

"We'd all appreciate it, miss, if you could fix up the gals," he'd said, avoiding her eyes. "Affecting the cowhands and the other workers. Doc Smith ain't having any luck with his remedies."

So she was trekking through the Sonoran desert, up and down ravines, into the most lightning-struck area on God's brown earth, to un-hex a bordello full of whores so cowpokes wouldn't lose what they were doing their pokin' with.

The heavens opened up like someone dumped a chamber pot full of hot piss on her head, soaking her hat, her moth-eaten serape (another gift from the rancher, since she'd also lost her good wool coat to the Ix-hunpedzkins), and her cotton shirt underneath.

Figured.

Malyu plodded on, flicking raindrops from her long ears.

Until a fork of lightning zapped right in front of them, splitting a tall saguaro into two with a crash that reverberated through her skull, raising her hair and Malyu's brushy mane straight up, spotting her eyesight with stars.

Rather than bolting like a scatterbrained horse, Malyu stopped cold, bracing her legs and flattening her ears. Good. They could both recover for a few minutes.

A squawk like a pissed off chicken blasted her ears just as her hearing was coming back. Wind whipped around her, tossing her hat off her head. Her ears ringing, Dinah looked around, trying to see anything but white spots. Unflappable Malyu trembled beneath her legs.

Another squawk, this time more curious, softer. Dinah squinted.

Big. Big as Malyu. Bigger. Shoot, the damn head was as big as Malyu.

A thunderbird. Raptor's beak half open, hawklike head cocked, lightning-filled eyes on hers. One clawed foot wrapped around the charred steaming saguaro, bent to the ground, the other on a brown granite boulder shot with quartzite.

Not that it needed anything to stand on to have the advantage of high ground. Two feet on the ground and it'd still tower over her and Malyu.

It stretched its wings, knocking down another saguaro, then tucked them tightly against its body.

Did it look abashed? Dinah didn't even have a moment to consider if it was sorry about the saguaro when Malyu decided *enough*, ducking her head and bucking Dinah off.

Straight towards a thicket of cholla, their short stubby branches yearning towards her flying body.

Til something grabbed at her collar, bloodying her neck, catching her before she landed.

The cholla huffed in disappointment, seemed like, as Dinah dangled from the thunderbird's beak.

"Put me down, you overgrown chicken!"

The thunderbird chuffed in surprise and dropped her, thank the seven gods, *away* from the cholla. Dinah scrambled up, grabbed her hat and dusted it off, then turned to face the creature.

Who did look a bit like a chicken, all hunkered down like it was now, cream and pale gray feathers matted by the torrential rain, lambent blue eyes intent on her face, head tilted and beak agape. Not the brightest look.

Then the thunderbird chirped, sharp staccato tweets that suited a sparrow, not the huge beast in front of her.

She knew she should be terrified, that its beak could pluck off her fool head. But there it was, puffed all up like a baby bird wanting a meal from its mama. Just curious.

Even Malyu was relaxing, head down, one rear foot cocked, occasionally nibbling on a tuft of straw-like grass, nearly asleep despite the downpour and flashes of lightning and crashes of thunder and a predatory bird big as a caboose just sittin' there.

"Don't you be scarin' me or my mule," Dinah scolded. "Or knocking over the saguaros."

The thunderbird ducked its head. Why, it *was* just a baby.

If it was baby-sized, just how big were the parents? Dinah didn't know anyone who'd seen a thunderbird this close up. Normally they flew so high you couldn't rightly tell their size. And they were rare. A person was lucky to see them once or twice in their lifetime.

And here was one just sittin' in front of her, fluffing its feathers as the rain slowed up.

Its feathers. Its feathers, infused with magic and monsoons.

Just one feather, *one*, would sell for enough gold for her to replenish her amulet store, then some. And if she could keep a second for herself? Who knew what she could craft, given time and study. An amulet to let her fly, to channel the lightnings, to control a storm?

She couldn't help herself, she reached her hand out—

—then yanked it back. *Never* take, never, her mama had always told her, and Dinah never had. Only receive what is freely (or at least contractually) given. Or what you've won. Or....well, Dinah was no innocent. But she played fair, and she'd never hurt something without provocation. Never stolen anything from someone who'd not stolen it already from someone else.

She reached out again, but this time just to stroke that fearsome hooked baby beak, black as obsidian, big as Malyu's head. The beak was dusty where it joined skin. She polished it, rubbing til that section gleamed too. The chick closed its eyes and leaned towards her. Dinah scritched up under its chin, digging her fingers into warm downy fluff, and it warbled softly, spreading its wings a little so she could scratch under there, too.

It smelled good, like fresh rain and the desert abloom. Creosote and sage and wet limestone.

The thunderheads blew out, and the moon showed her pale face.

Dinah didn't know how long she'd cuddled up to the thunderbird chick, but Malyu was asleep, ears twitching, and Dinah's serape was warm and dry. The cholla scars had faded from her hand. She felt good, restored, healed. Best she felt in weeks.

A shadow blotted the moon, then flew on owl-silent wings to land next to her and the chick.

Half again as big as the chick, the adult thunderbird mantled, black and white striped and speckled wings, fully the length of several train cars, spread and cupped, and glared at her with opalescent, black-pupilled eyes.

Dinah sure hoped it wasn't going to eat her. Or Malyu, who still dozed. Only time she'd seen a hawk or eagle arch its wings like that was when it was guarding its food.

It trilled at the chick, who raised its head sleepily and chirped back. The adult looked at the chick, looked at Dinah, then nestled up next to its baby and began preening the chick's feathers.

Dinah let out the breath she didn't know she was holding.

Don't presume. A wry male voice echoed in her brain. *You're just lucky Tł'é'na'áí likes you.* He snapped his beak at her, smirking as she jerked back.

She didn't know how she knew he was smirking. She just did.

....feathers, hmmm? he said.

"I'm sorry. But I didn't take one."

Or two. He considered her. *Pretty hair. Shiny. Braid me a bracelet I can attach to my collection.* He jiggled his left leg. A worn leather band was knotted around it, with a small embroidered doeskin pouch attached to it.

She shrugged. It wasn't safe to give pieces of yourself away, but did she have a choice? She unbound her hair, letting it cascade down her back. Glossy black, with a scant handful of silver streaking it at her temples, it gleamed in the moonlight.

Faster than she could blink, the thunderbird snaked his head at her and ripped out a hank.

"You rotten—"

Braid, he commanded. *I just did what you thought of.*

"And *didn't* do!" Tears stung her eyes. That *hurt.* He hadn't grabbed a lot, but blood dotted the roots, smearing across the strands as she braided. He had snagged a fair amount of silver, so she carefully wove that in to contrast most with the black.

She went over to Malyu and yanked a few hairs off her tail. Malyu didn't care. Didn't even wake up.

Dinah wrapped either end of her braid with Malyu's tougher hair.

"There," she said, holding it out. *Now you can find me wherever I go.*

So much more than that, he thought back, regarding the bracelet. *But thank you. Nicely done. Tuck it into my pouch, please.*

Now, he continued, *I rarely get to speak to one of you two-legged creatures. Tell me of your world.*

She told him about her travels. Her adventures, her jobs, as a sorceress for hire. The sweet little jackrabbit girl she left behind a year ago, the crafty fox sorcerer who nearly killed her before that. And finally, her voice husky with sorrow, she spoke about her Chinese sorceress mama and college professor pa, dead these many years, and just how much she missed having someone who loved her, no matter what.

"They never even thought how alone I'd be. How I'd never fit in, anywhere. Half Chinese, half white. They just loved each other. Loved me. But they never expected to get sick and just die. No one ever thinks that. Then they're gone, beyond all worry or care. Never mind the folks they leave behind."

He absently preened her hair as she spoke, interjecting only rarely. Just listening.

She spoke til she fell asleep, cuddled up between him and his chick.

THE CLATTER of hooves on hard packed earth woke her. A herd of javelina, pungently musky, nosed around her and Malyu, then scattered when she sat up, little tails wagging as they trotted off on their dainty feet.

The thunderbirds were gone.

She touched the penny-sized spot where the thunderbird had yanked out her hair. It no longer ached. Wasn't even scabbed over. And there was hair, already re-grown, long enough she could tug it in front of her face. Not her normal glossy black, or even the ever increasing silver, but a sparkling bluish white. Lightning-struck.

The morning sun kissed the peaks to the east, warming the violet shadows cast by the saguaros. It rose swiftly, chasing away the chill of the night.

And highlighted two feathers, one cream and gray, the other striped black and white, sitting by her hat.

THE GOD TOUCHED PREACHER MAN

The preacher man's dimly lit white clapboard house, set behind the white plastered adobe Church of the Sons of the Army of the Lord, stank of cats.

Cats. So many cats. Gray cats, tabby cats, fat cats, skinny cats. Lounging on the preacher man's battered oak bookcase, on the pair of parlour chairs, and on the scratched up spindle-legged settee. Trotting across the smooth pine floor. Staring at Dinah with suspicious lambent eyes of gold and green.

Dinah joined three felines (a female tuxedo, an orange and white tom, and a young white kitten) on the settee, gently squeezing in between them. They shifted reluctantly.

She touched the frayed wool of the cushions, rough against her fingertips. Used to be smooth, she bet. Til those little fiends used it to sharpen their claws.

Smelled like they did their business inside, not outside as was proper.

At least there weren't any mice.

Dinah breathed shallowly, mouth slightly agape, hoping she didn't look like the mayor's son, kicked in the head by a mule when he was a child of seven years, and brain addled ever since, poor child. She *needed* this job. Needed some cash.

As a young sorceress with a muddled ancestry, making her own way through this magnificent desolate land, only her wits and her meager powers kept herself fed and safe.

The preacher man, all skinny limbs and protruding eyes and an Adam's apple you could hang your hat on, sat on a rough wooden stool in front of her. A fat brown tabby draped across his lap, licking one plush paw. The cat nudged his hands and he scratched behind her ears.

That's how you do it, human, her half-lidded emerald eyes said.

The white kitten, poking at Dinah's amulet pouch, dug out her prize possession: a black-and-white striped thunderbird wing feather. The adult male thunderbird had left it for her, a gift after an evening of tales and warmth last summer in the Sonoran Desert between himself, his son, and her.

In that short time, he became a second father to her. She would always have a home with him and his family, though they weren't her species.

The feather was a memory of, for once, not being alone. Of maybe having a home.

The kitten chewed on the feather while shredding the barbs with his needlelike claws.

No. Just *no*. Dinah liked cats, she did, but they needed to learn boundaries like every other creature.

Dinah took the feather away, tucking it back into her pouch, then scritched behind the white kitten's ears.

It swatted her hand, drawing beads of blood.

So that's how it was.

She deposited the kitten on the floor. It glared at her, then scampered off.

"Something ain't right," Reverend Robert Orrin Smith finally said, wringing his long bony hands. "I've been hexed. I've prayed to the Lord for help, and he sent you."

"What's been going on?" Dinah asked in her soft husky voice, after surreptitiously wiping the blood on her kerchief.

"Visions," he said. "Visions that come to me, night and day, visions of horrible creatures, demons, infesting our town. Devouring our stores. Devouring *us*.

"I've always been a Godly man," he continued. "But I will admit, one of my sins is that I always wanted to be especially blessed and favored by our Lord. Before now, I would have welcomed visions, visions from God. But these, though they seem to be in warning, do not come from the Lord. I can't sleep. I can barely eat. I'm ready to slice my own wrists to stop the torment, though that would doom me to Hell.

"I know the Lord lets some folks suffer, but I do not think He would let this happen, not to me, his faithful servant.

"And I have never had a vision in the Church proper. During one vision, I stumbled through the doorway into the church. It was like a knife cut clean through my mind, and I could see, not the horrors advancing, with fat bellies and blood-soaked fur and yellowed teeth, but the morning light purely shining through the church window, illuminating the pulpit. A balm to my soul.

"If these visions were truly from God, why would entering the church stop them?"

Dinah considered.

"I don't know if what you're suffering is a hex, Reverend Smith. Sounds more like someone or something is communicating with you. Warning you. I'll find the perpetrator, for the fee we discussed. That I promise you."

THE TOWN of Blueacre sprawled along the valley floor next to Blue's Peak and the Blue Ribbon Mine. The Blue Ribbon Mine was legendary, initially producing veins of pure silver, next thick ribbons of gold, and finally diamonds big as a tall man's fist and blue as the noonday sky, the deeper the miners dug. Now she'd heard they'd found a new metal, bright as sunlight, strong as steel.

Maybe once Blueacre was an acre big, when silver was the only substance the mine produced. Now it sprawled, covering enough ground to boast several bordellos, five saloons, three hotels and a scattering of boarding houses, and even segregated areas for the Chinese, Natives, and everyone else. Dinah herself had rented a pleasant, sun-drenched room on the top floor of the boarding house on the far edge of town.

Dinah headed straight for the Chinese quarter after her meeting with Reverend Smith. Half Chinese, half white, and not passing in either society, she could at least avail herself of a source of information closed to white folks.

The quarter was quiet. No one hawked their wares, or girls, or poppy. No one chit chatted over washing or ironing or mending laundry. No old men mixed up foul concoctions to fix whatever disease the gals passed on or the flux someone caught drinking tainted water.

Dinah strode through empty side streets, dodging the rare furtive glance or subdued invitation.

She was looking for someone like *her*. A sorceress, or at least a sorcerer. Someone who might have noticed anything or anyone strange. Someone wary and smart.

Picking her way amongst the puddles of mud and crowded one-story rough log cabins, she caught the scent of sweet spicy meat, savory noodles, and pungent vegetables. Hunger poked her belly. It'd been weeks since she'd eaten anyone's cooking beside her own sorry attempts on the trail.

She found the source of the cooking, a small courtyard with a fireplace and roaring cook fire, steel pots dangling over the flames. No one tended the food. One ramshackle wooden table and bench sat near the fireplace. The courtyard was enclosed by other buildings, except for the narrow passage into it.

The rich scent of meat intensified. Smelled like something her mama had cooked for her when she was a little girl. Noodles and sweet roasted pork.

Dinah's watch-out amulet, a small contraption of silver wire interwoven with hairs from her mule Malyu's mane, tucked underneath her loose fitting cotton blouse, jabbed her between her breasts. Dinah had worn it on a deer leather thong around her neck for the past several months. It had never reacted before.

"Would you walk into my parlour?" a soft voice said from beside her.

Dinah turned. A petite woman, shorter than Dinah by a head, dressed in a mishmash of red Chinese silk robes and hard wearing black cotton skirts, stood in the shadow of a silk curtain-draped doorway.

"I am Lei Ming," the woman said. She looked young, younger than Dinah's twenty-five years, with smooth ivory skin and delicate features. Her eyes were moonless night black, the dark irises spangled by silver flecks.

Her eyes were ancient.

"I'm looking for a bit of information," Dinah said. She wiped at her mouth. "I ain't so easy to ensnare, Madam Lei. You can save the bait for someone else."

Lei Ming smiled sweetly. "It is already cooked. It shouldn't go to waste. Come inside and we will talk. You can enjoy some of the meat."

Still Dinah hesitated.

"Come, silly girl, I will not harm you," Lei Ming said. She ducked under the curtain and into the dark cabin, taking tiny light steps. Golden lotus feet under those long skirts, Dinah guessed. Tortured into exquisite fashion.

Dinah followed her.

The room they entered into was actually a narrow hallway, with steep earthen steps carved into the darkness. Hundreds of steps. Impossible. How deep into the earth did they lead?

"Hurry, silly girl!" called Lei Ming, so far below she was a tiny silhouette holding a torch, with a cold blue flame flickering at the tip. The rough-hewn walls glittered with streaks of silver.

Dinah stepped down, slipping a bit on the sandy steps. She'd wanted to find a sorceress. She didn't figure she'd find one so skilled, so far beyond her, but that's what the dumbass coyote thought when he grabbed a turkey's tailfeather and ended up with the wingtip of a thunderbird.

Ten, twenty, fifty steps, and all of sudden Lei Ming was standing right in front of her, at the entrance to a wide circular chamber with a sky blue painted ceiling high overhead. Torches in iron holders affixed to the rough stone walls lit the chamber with warm flickering firelight. Silk and wool tapestries, mounted between the torches, depicted brilliantly colored dragons in a wide range of habitats. The tapestries covered a semicircle's worth of wall space. Wooden crates sat against the bare wall opposite.

The floor was polished celadon jade. A heavily carved rosewood table sat in the center of the chamber, the legs of the table sinuous dragons. Dragons also adorned the blocky wooden chairs, writhing down the legs and along the backs. There was no other furniture.

If Dinah looked sideways through narrowed eyes, she could see the dragons on the tapestries shifting to more closely watch her.

"Sit," ordered Lei Ming, rustling her skirts and sitting down herself.

Dinah didn't argue. She hoped the chair and table dragons weren't as mobile and the tapestry dragons.

A servant slipped from behind the tapestry embroidered with a Celestial Dragon, carrying an iron teapot and two pale green porcelain cups on a lacquered tray. Two Pekingese dogs, one cream, one jet black, followed him into the chamber, then trotted to Ling Mei.

The servant placed the tray on the table between them, bowed, and retreated.

"Pour, child," Lei Ming said, reaching down to fondle the ears of the cream Pekingese.

Dinah did so, careful not to spill, filling both cups. The scent of jasmine tea, sweet and floral, enveloped her. She offered a cup to Lei Ming, who accepted it graciously, and sipped.

Dinah took a healthy swig herself. It was fresh and light and wafted away her trepidation.

"Do you know Reverend Robert Smith?" Dinah asked.

Lei Ming nodded. "I do. Enthusiastic, but kind. Naive. He has a rather distasteful affinity for felines." The black Peke yapped.

"He's been having ungodly visions of demons, creatures, invading Blueacre."

"Do you really think the sender of the visions ungodly?" Ling Mei asked. "Or simply not of his Christian god?"

"I don't care one way or the other," Dinah admitted. "I promised to find who or what is sending the visions."

"Many foreign gods and goddesses travel through Deseret in these days. You should be more concerned about the *why*, not the *who*," said Ling Mei. "Men have dug deeply, here, far deeper than they should have. Disturbing things best left to rest, opening passages normally closed."

The servant reappeared, placing a porcelain plate of noodles and pink roasted pork in front of Dinah, then handed her a bleached linen napkin and a pair of chopsticks. He bowed.

Rather than leave the room this time, he walked to the nearest tapestry and gently removed it from the wall, folded it, and placed it in one of the wooden crates. He proceeded to the next, and the next, til all the tapestry dragons slumbered in the crates.

"You're leaving," Dinah said. "All the Chinese. That's why it's so damned quiet."

"Eat your noodles, child. They shouldn't go to waste, and you'll need your strength."

"Something is coming," Dinah said. "Something that's scared off even one as powerful as you. You won't stay and fight for your home?"

Ling Mei's eyes narrowed. Her shadow shifted behind her, lengthening and twisting into that of a sinuous winged dragon. "This is not, and would never be, *home*."

Dinah detected a bit of sulfur, saw a wisp of smoke trail from one finely sculpted nostril. Her mama had taught her not to poke at dangerous creatures, when Dinah was just a little girl watching her mama conjure salamanders.

She hadn't learned that lesson very well, Dinah admitted to

herself, rubbing one of the shiny white burn scars on her hand. Ah well.

Dinah stabbed a chunk of pork with the tip of a chopstick. "Your cook is skilled," she said, slurping up some noodles next.

Lei Ming composed herself, her shadow shrinking to human size. "I cooked it myself," she said.

"Why, thank you, then," Dinah said. She finished her plateful of food. "Best meal I've had in I don't even recall how long."

"You'll need your strength. And your pluck," Lei Ming said sourly. "Know this: you are far stronger than you believe. Trust that, when the time is right."

"Have you seen what's coming?"

Lei Ming looked down at her cup of tea, then met Dinah's eyes. Lei Ming's starry eyes brimmed with fear.

"I have."

~

DINAH CARRIED a canvas bag full of supplies: a pouch of gunpowder, a roll of waxed cotton cord, blasting caps, and a dozen sticks of dynamite. A gift from Madam Lei.

"Collapse the mine," Madam Lei had whispered. "Don't wait too long. Tonight. The moon will be dark, but you don't have time to wait for a more auspicious moment."

Tonight might be too late. Madam Lei didn't have to tell her that. Dinah had doubted Smith's words, thinking he truly was beset by an enemy, that the visions weren't true. That she could find the person responsible.

But she trusted the visions of Madam Lei, trusted the honor of dragons. Reverend Smith's visions were real.

Soon as she'd climbed the stairs out of Madam Lei's chamber and winded through the narrow streets of the abandoned Chinese section she could feel little beady eyes staring at her from the shadows, could hear the hissing and chittering of creatures just the other side of the

Dream World. She shuddered. Reached for her thunderbird feather, stroked it, let the memories calm her.

Madam Lei had left through the servant's passageway, Pekingese dogs at her heels. Dinah wasn't even sure if that passageway exited into Blueacre, or if it somehow led to Madam Lei's true home in faraway China.

Dinah was on her own. Maybe Reverend Smith would help her. But she didn't know what he could do. He didn't strike her as a man of action.

She couldn't argue with anyone that destroying the mine *wouldn't* destroy the town. It would. If anyone caught wind of her plan, she'd be strung up quicker than that white kitten had swatted her.

No one would believe the visions of a bumbling preacher man or a Chinese dragon sorceress. Certainly no one would believe her, a half Chinese woman who dressed like a man.

No one would believe that soon, demons would kill everyone in Blueacre.

It was midafternoon by the time Dinah rode her mule Malyu to Reverend Smith's house.

She'd packed up all her meager belongings. She'd paid for a week at the boarding house, but didn't think she'd be going back. Prudence dictated she prepare for the worst possibility, and that meant high-tailing it out of Blueacre soon as she collapsed the mine.

But she had promised Preacher Smith she'd find out who sent him his visions.

She heard a thunking and moaning from inside the clapboard house. She looped Malyu's reins over the porch railing, opened the door, and ran in, running past the cats staring at her with worried eyes, til she reached the small bedroom tucked into the back of the house.

Reverend Smith thrashed atop the iron bed, hands batting at unseen foes, his back arching, wailing to wake the dead.

He collapsed, face streaked with sweat and tears, against the worn flour sack quilt.

The fat brown tabby leapt up next to his head, licking his chin, his cheeks, even one of his eyelids, til Reverend Smith opened the opposite eye and stroked her soft striped head. "Now, now, Betsy," he murmured.

"What did you see, Reverend Smith?" Dinah whispered.

"Blood pooling in the streets. Everyone dead. The buildings burning. And an unholy darkness rolling out of the mine." Betsy chirped and snuggled closer. "Is this real, Miss Dinah? Or am I going crazy? I knew a man who preached up north. He had visions til his eyes skewed in his skull and he suffered a seizure and died. I know I should be brave, and trust the Lord, but Miss Dinah, I am terribly afraid for either myself, if indeed the visions are an aberration of my brain, or all of Blueacre, every man, woman, and child, if what I see is true."

"What you see *is* the truth to come, Reverend Smith. Someone who loves you has been trying to warn you." She eyed the brown tabby Betsy. "And those terrible things will happen, unless you and I change fate. And I have a plan. But you have to help me ensure its success."

She grasped his hand, helped him sit up. "Can you do that, Reverend Smith?"

～

Once you entered the earth, it was always night. Miners didn't only work during the day. But fewer worked through the evening hours, and Dinah would sacrifice them to save the rest of the town.

"It's safer to blow the mine now," she told Smith as she loosely tethered Malyu.

Smith had harnessed a mare he'd rented to an old farm cart and piled all the cats into the cart. He fumbled with the rope hobble til Dinah yanked it away and secured the mare. He was lucky the mare didn't bite or kick him.

The mine was a quarter mile up the rocky slope. Though the cart could handle the rutted road, Dinah wanted a bit of distance between the mine and Malyu and Smith's mare, should the worst happen.

'Course, if the demons did get out of the mine, Malyu would still be between the mine and Blueacre.

Dinah added, "I don't know how much time we have."

Reverend Smith refused. "They are children of God, and ours are not the hands that should smite them. They are innocent."

Dinah doubted that. It was the miners' greed that led them to dig so deeply, to thin the barrier between the true world and the Dream World.

She agreed to an hour, no more, for him to enter the mine with his cats, to get the miners out. Dinah believed the cats understood the risk, and accepted it. Each cat had submitted, under Betsy's watchful eyes, to a minor cantrip enabling them to speak words of warning.

If nothing else, the miracle of a cat speaking might surprise the miners enough to get them moving.

Dinah had never entered a mine before. She expected a tidy passageway, framed by timber, heading deep into the mountain. Even a mine car on steel rails.

The actuality was a warren of narrow passages and plummeting drops, navigable only by ropes or ladders and chalked symbols on the rough-hewn stone walls. Or by agile footed felines.

Cats scurried down each passageway, eyes reflecting the light from the kerosene lanterns. Smith kept to the main passageway, Betsy trotting at his side.

God-damned, God-touched preacher man. *Goddess*-touched, rather. Dinah hoped the cat would keep him safe.

Dinah laid out the cotton cord and attached the blasting caps to the cord and the sticks of dynamite as Madam Lei had instructed, placing dynamite at the beginning of the main passageway, the next two largest, and at the opening to the mine itself. She trailed the lines of cord to just outside the mine entrance.

Dinah invoked a *Don't-See-Me* amulet, dripping her own life's blood onto the brass disc and onto the blasting caps and dynamite.

She feared if she dampened the surface of the waxed cord it wouldn't burn like it should. She just hoped no one coming out would notice it.

She tucked herself behind a sandstone boulder and drank a bit of warm whiskey from her flask. Stroked her thunderbird feather for comfort.

It was cold since the sun tucked behind the mountains.

Now she had to wait, wait as long as she could. According to her papa's pocket watch, she had only another half hour of the time she promised Reverend Smith.

Another quarter hour and cats began spilling out of the mine entrance, followed by a handful of bemused miners. Not as many as she expected were still in the depths of the mine. She kept herself hidden, not wanting to push the power of the don't-see-me amulet, hoping that twilight would hide the cords until the miners cleared the area.

One miner tripped close enough for her to reach out and tap his nose. He was a young black man, his wooly hair pulled back into a tail, his cheekbones stark under deep-set eyes.

She held her breath.

"Gosh darn it," he muttered, standing up, not bothering to dust himself off. "Clumsy fool. Cat, where you get going to? Cat, come back here!"

A dainty buff colored cat with dark paws and face sauntered back to him.

"Danger," the cat said, her voice raspy. "Come with me if you would live. Danger." She twitched her tail, and he followed her.

Dinah breathed.

Five minutes. The pack of miners was heading down the mountain, herded by the magicked cats.

Three.

One.

Reverend Smith tore out of the entrance, blood streaking down his face from a rent in his cheek. He clutched Betsy in his arms, close to his chest.

The fat tabby, her fur blood-soaked, wasn't moving.

"Blow it, Miss Dinah, for the love all that's holy, blow it NOW!"

Dinah struck a match against the sandstone. A whiff of sulfur soured her nostrils, but the match didn't catch. She struck another, and another. More sulfur.

No flames.

And the sulfur wasn't all from the ripped match heads. A yellow cloud of sulfur and methane belched from the mine entrance. She could see shapes, vicious shadows, within the cloud.

Gods above, she was going to die here on this ruined rocky ground.

She dug in her amulet pouch. She didn't have any fire-starting amulets. Why bother, when mundane matches sufficed? But surely, surely there was something she could use...and her traitorous heart whimpered, *more blood to the* Don't-See-Me *amulet.*

No. That was simply not an option.

She touched the soft downy barbs at the base of the thunderbird feather. This feather was precious, more precious than gold, or blue diamonds, or Dream World metals. The thunderbird was a father of her heart, of her choosing, and this was her physical tie to him.

But it wasn't worth more than the lives of the miners, or of the cats, or the townspeople.

Or of Reverend Smith, cradling Betsy's limp body against his chest, his eyes desperate as he shouted at her, running like molasses had trapped his legs.

She would sacrifice the feather.

And herself, if it came to that.

And it might.

She'd never channeled the lightnings before. Didn't know if any mortal human ever had.

But she had to try.

You are stronger than you believe, whispered Madam Lei.

Dinah ran to the front of the mine entrance. Palms out, thunderbird feather tucked between her thumb and index finger, she faced the mine entrance as the demons boiled out.

Braced herself.

She *called* the lightning, summoning it out of the sunset sky, using the feather as her focus. The barbs glowed, so hot they arced blue.

And the lightning came.

The lightning struck through her, through her skull, along her veins, and out through her palms.

She guided it even as sizzling tears streamed down her cheeks, incinerating the creatures as they raced to her. The bolts blasted through the entrance at the masses teeming inside.

As they howled and burned, as the stench of burning flesh billowed out of the cave entrance, Dinah raised her hands to at the rocky slope above, using the lightning to collapse the slope across the mine's entrance.

Even if any survived her lightning, nothing could dig or blast through that chunk of mountain.

Detonations, the dynamite finally catching and exploding within the mine, rattled Dinah's skull as she let the lightnings die.

Dinah collapsed.

Cool rough hands pressed against her head.

"You just can't help yourself, can you, darlin'," a rough voice said.

Coyote.

"And you just can't help but find anything excuse to get your paws on me," Dinah said hoarsely, pushing him away and sitting up. He was in his coyote-headed half human form, his long pink tongue lolling in a canid laugh.

"Is that any way to thank someone for savin' your life?" he chided. "Don't keep pushin' it, darlin'. Soon you're gonna owe me more than you can ever repay."

"Didn't ask for this, old dog," she said.

"Fair enough," he said. "Guess I won't lay a claim for this time."

"Fair enough."

"Wake up, Dinah." He swiped her nose with his tongue.

REVEREND SMITH HAD MANAGED to get Dinah into his cart and Malyu tied to the back by the time Dinah opened her eyes.

She was surrounded by soft purring bundles of fur. The cats.

The rhythmic sound soothed her hurts all the way back to Blueacre.

BETSY WASN'T DEAD, just sore injured. But goddesses are made of sturdier stuff than mere cats or humans, and Betsy was kissing Reverend Smith's nose soon enough, comforting him as Dinah stitched up his torn open cheek.

"I couldn't get all the men out," he mumbled. "They refused to listen to me. Mocked me, saying I was a pansy-ass, lecturing to them as does real work. The demons came and slaughtered them. Knives for claws. I grabbed Betsy and ran."

"You did what you could," Dinah said quietly. "The cats got some folks out. I expect that some of those cats will have new homes."

Dinah painted his cheek with a healing ointment, thick with willow, sage, and mint, then applied some to her blistered palms.

"You know, Reverend Smith, you can't stay here. The only ones that saw the demons are us and the dead. The townspeople will not be thankful that you saved them from things they can't understand and won't believe. If they think you had anything, anything at all, to do with the destruction of the mine... they're gonna blame someone, and who has all the cats? And who's been going around talking about death and destruction?"

"I can't rightly blame them," Reverend Smith said, stroking Betsy, who snuggled against him and purred. "There's nothing else here for this town but the mine."

"I'm traveling to Salt Lake City. You're welcome to come with. You and, um, Betsy."

"One thing you never figured out. Who sent those visions to me, Miss Dinah?"

Dinah paused and glanced at Betsy. Bastet, mayhap? Not plain old Betsy? The cat stared back, then slowly squinted one emerald eye at her.

A wink?

Betsy did it again.

Well, alright then.

"Reverend, I know you're a pious man of God, but you do understand in this world of ours, your God isn't the only one?"

Smith dug in his pocket, handed her a small blue diamond, clear as the noonday sky. "Go on, Miss Dinah."

So she did, telling him of the gods of the ancient worlds and the new, those beings of power and knowledge. Coyote. Crow. Raven.

And Bastet, goddess of cats, protector of the home.

Betsy purred.

THE LOST CHILDREN

Dinah trailed her fingers over the worn spines of the books, dim sunlight streaming through the wavy glass windows highlighting the titles.

Algebra, Latin, geography (both of the United States and of Europe). Webster's Speller. All four McGuffey's Readers, smelling of new ink. A complete collection of the works of Aristotle, the titles blurred. Shakespeare, Richard the Third.

Her favorite, that one was. She stroked the spine, then dropped her hand.

She hadn't seen so many books in one place since she sold her parent's belongings after their deaths from yellow fever. It'd broken her heart to sell her papa's library, but a travelling sorceress with just one mule, not even an additional packhorse, couldn't carry around chests of books.

Never mind that no one expected a half-Chinese woman to be able to read.

She hoped, inhaling the dry warmth of the texts, that her papa's books had found a home like this little schoolhouse in Boot Hill City. Where they'd be loved and used.

It was Sunday, and none of the children were in class. Some of them would be in church with their parents. Others worked, doing chores around their homes.

And some of them were missing. Taken.

Which was why Dinah was here.

"Would you like some tea, Miss Dinah?" the school teacher, Miss Caroline Bordelon, asked. She'd put a kettle on the pot belly stove as soon as Dinah had walked in. Only Dinah's sharp eyes caught the trembling in Miss Bordelon's hands.

Exhaustion and fear would do that to a woman.

Miss Bordelon was younger than Dinah, with wavy dark hair pinned up over soft features. A few curls escaped, tracing her wide cheekbones. She was the type of woman a young child would run for comfort, with a broad bosom and strong arms. Her skin was the color of water-soaked oak, rich gold brown, absorbing the sunlight for its own. Her voice was sweet and slow, luscious as snowberry honey, with a soft drawling accent Dinah couldn't place, but thought she could listen to all day.

If little lives weren't at risk.

"Tea would be lovely." Dinah figured she had a lot of asking questions to do.

Miss Bordelon poured tea into two chipped porcelain cups. Bergamot infused the small room.

"Sugar?"

Dinah's mouth watered. "Yes, thank you."

"Does the boarding house suit?" Miss Bordelon asked. "My room is just down the hall from yours. Please knock if you require anything. Mrs Daniels cooks up a lovely breakfast, and she'll pack you a meal for mid day if you require it. Supper is plain, but filling."

Dinah sipped her tea, letting the sweetness sting her teeth. "Miss Bordelon, thank you for the tea"—and the precious sugar!—"but let's just get to the point.

"You have three missing children from this town. No trace of 'em anywhere. And they disappeared after leaving your schoolhouse, before they reached home." Dinah settled back on top of one of the children's desks, flicking off a glistening green grasshopper before she squashed it. "Tell me about the children."

HER FRIEND GEORGE KINMAN, a black cowboy who owned the livery stable in Boot Hill, had sought her out in the matter of the missing children. *No one else seemed to care*, he wrote in the letter carried by a raven hexed to deliver it. *Could she help*?

She'd ridden up from Salt Lake City as fast as she could coax her mule Malyu over the passes, arriving in town late last night.

Three children, aged five through ten. Male and female, white and mixed. One bright, one earnest, one who just didn't give a pig's corkscrew tailed behind about school.

The only commonality between the children themselves?

"They were not wanted by their families," Miss Bordelon said. "I think, in two of the cases, the parents are happy to be rid of the burden. In the last, they are frustrated that they've lost a servant, nothing more."

"And taken on the afternoon of the dark of the moon," Dinah mused, on her third cup of sugar-sweetened tea. "Lots of unsavory creatures favor the time when the moon can't see them. Maybe scenting the hurt those kids suffered."

"Or maybe just the darkness gave courage to someone who decided to help," Miss Bordelon said. "Maybe those children are in a better place."

"Did you spirit those children away, Miss Bordelon?" Dinah asked.

"I did not." Miss Bordelon stared at her fiercely. "I love those children like they were my own, like their families should have. But I did not take them away. Even when Jimmy Wright came in with a broken arm, or Octavia Miller with her face swollen and bruised.

"I wish I had, but I didn't. I can only hope that they are somewhere safe."

"Chances of that aren't so good, Miss Bordelon. You know that."

Miss Bordelon's posture remained erect, but her soft voice slumped. "I know that, Miss Dinah, I do.

"And it's only two more nights before the dark of the moon. I fear I'll lose another, Dinah, and that I can't abide."

DINAH MET George Kinman for mid day dinner at the saloon. Last time she'd seen him was when she was helping her papa's friend Jack Robertson figure out who was despoiling his water sources. Kinman had moved to the Deseret Territories after the War between the States. He had a gentle hand with horses and a soft heart for anything helpless.

She spotted him across the dim saloon, tucked away at a table in the corner, far from the clink of glasses and conversation at the bar. She wove her way through the small noonday crowd, bumping into an elderly Native man. He was dressed in a mix of Native and white attire, with a woven fiber basket on his back, and rested his weight on two canes.

"Excuse me, Grandfather," she apologized. He nodded stiffly at her, black eyes reflecting a chitinous glimmer, then shuffled away.

She sat across from Kinman, swatting a couple grasshoppers off the stained pine tabletop. The barkeeper placed plates of beef and potatoes in front of them. The potatoes swam in a cream sauce. The slices of beef, rich and bloody, were dotted with flecks of herbs. A few caramelized pieces of roasted carrots and radishes finished out the plates.

"Fancy," Dinah said, poking at the beef.

"Owner's wife is French. Says we need a bit of culture here in Boot Hill," Kinman said, mouth full of potato and carrots. "It's good to see you, Dinah."

"You still rounding up herds of mustangs, George?"

He smiled. "Sure thing. Just not as often. I'm getting old, Dinah. My knees just can't take it like they used to. Once every couple years is enough. Thinking of teaching one of the men how to do it."

George would infiltrate a herd of mustangs, all slow and sneaky and gentle, til he identified the lead mare and won her trust. Rest of the herd would just follow him home. It wasn't magic. Just patience and kindness.

"I can train 'em still. The horses. They make good cowhorses." George stretched out his legs, wincing.

It wasn't just his knees, Dinah thought. The man had suffered terribly as a child in Kentucky, before being sold down the river to suffer more. That suffering wears a body out.

"Miss Bordelon is both helpful and not," Dinah said, getting to the matter at hand. "But I fear another child will be lost, if the pattern holds true. She told me the children taken were unloved, unwanted. Do you think that is important?"

"Only in that they are vulnerable," Kinman said. "Weakest in the herd. Maybe more willin' to go with someone offering a better life."

"Little Jimmy would come to the stable after school. Wanted to learn everything about the horses. I was thinking of askin' his family if he could be apprenticed to me."

"I'm sorry, George," Dinah said, taking his hand. "I truly am. I'll find who's taking the children, I promise."

SHE SPENT the next day and a half talking to the parents and plotting with George and Miss Bordelon. One of the lost children, Betty McNair, was an orphan, living with her grandparents. *Had been* living with her grandparents. They were tired, and poor. One less mouth to feed was a blessing they didn't want to feel thankful for, but did. The other families, inured to the loss of children in a harsh world, didn't feel any different.

Dinah understood that. Didn't like it, but understood it. She knew how blessed she had been, to have parents who loved her. So many children died, of disease and accidents, that to lose an unwanted child to design wasn't something those families mourned.

After supper Dinah went to the schoolhouse. Miss Bordelon,

leaning against her pine desk, chalk-dusted hands clasped in front of her, was just finishing up the final lesson for the youngest children, telling the story of Coyote trying to save the Moon from drowning in a well.

"And then the Moon glimmered, all soft light and giggles, while looking down at Coyote, splashing around in that well at her reflection. Laughing because he always rushed in, never checking first to see what was real and what wasn't." Mrs Bordelon stood up, long black cotton skirt swishing around the ankles of her boots. "Now, we're always gonna think twice, right, children? Caution is a virtue. Remember the other tales I told you today. Of Big Owl stealing children. Of Haakapainiži, old man Grasshopper, snatching up children and stuffing them into his basket. Of skinwalkers killing everyone for their skin, just for the fun of it."

The children chorused in agreement, jostling each other. Dinah smirked. She'd had her run ins with Coyote, and that tale sounded just like him.

"I've asked the children to go home at least partways together, the older taking care of younger," Miss Bordelon said to Dinah, watching the children put on their coats. "That just leaves the two I mentioned to you the other day, that would be travellin' alone."

Miss Bordelon gestured to two young girls, about 8 or 9 years old, one with strawberry blonde braids, the other with mud brown, wearing flour-sack dresses, worn wool coats, and knitted half mitts. They were holding hands, fingers entwined, knuckles white.

Poor little rabbits.

"Lolly Pickton, Mary Blackham, come say hello to Miss Dinah. She's gonna keep you safe."

The two girls stepped forward, ducking their heads. "Thank you, Miss Dinah," the brunette, Mary, murmured.

"I'll keep you safe," Dinah said. "I promise. Now, do either of you girls know how to ride? Because Mr Kinman has picked out two fine steeds for you."

Dinah bustled the girls out the door, the bodies of grasshoppers crunching underfoot on the porch. The sun set early this close to winter. They had only an hour of sunlight, maybe less, remaining. George had saddled up two buckskin mustang geldings, small enough to be pony-sized, for the girls. Dinah had her trusty mule Malyu, and George, rifle strapped to his saddle, rode his pretty black Appaloosa mare Dipper.

Fishing into her pouch of amulets, Dinah drew forth two, one for each girl. She looped them over their necks.

"These are amulets of protection," Dinah said. "Now, I need to tune them to you, alright? I just need a drop of blood from each of you. Be brave!"

She pricked the thumbs of each girl with the tip of her ritual knife, a small sharp blade of silver she honed constantly, and smeared the blood onto each girl's amulet. Neither cried out, not even a whimper, though their eyes widened and both tensed. Little frozen rabbits. Dinah could see when the spell fired up. A dim warm glow emanated from the girls. It would only last a few hours, but that should give Dinah and George time to get the girls home. Dinah boosted each little girl into their saddles, then mounted Malyu.

"You know the way, George?" Dinah asked.

"Sure do. Mary first." He nudged Dipper into a trot. The two geldings followed, then Dinah.

"I'll meet you at the boarding house after," Dinah called back to Miss Bordelon.

DINAH PULLED out other amulets as they rode. *Protection* over the party, *See-Clearly* to penetrate illusions, *Strike-True* to guide any defensive shooting or stabbing on her part. She nicked the meat of her thumb and anointed each, then looped them around her neck. She touched the last Thunderbird feather she possessed, tucked safely into its own pouch, a striped wing feather from a juvenile Thunderbird, gifted to her after an evening of sharing and acceptance. For luck, and reassurance.

She could channel the lightnings through it if need be, though that would destroy the feather.

So be it.

She kept it clutched in one gloved hand, the other loosely holding Malyu's reins. Shoot, she could guide Malyu with her knees. She dropped the reins, tied ends keeping them from dangling, and pulled out her fighting knife, her yǎnyuèdāo. Her mama had gifted her the blade right before she died, ten inches of wicked hooked steel protruding from a Chinese dragon's mouth that topped the leather-wrapped hilt.

Steel and lightning. She was as prepared as she could be.

Mary's homestead lay to the east of Boot Hill City, down the mountain, through the chaparral and high dusty grasses, just starting to green with the winter moisture. A trickle of a creek provided a bit of water for the grazing sheep. Come spring it would be torrential with snow melt.

The three-mile ride to the homestead was quiet. Every quarter mile or so Dinah's neck prickled. The *See-Clearly* charm honed her eyesight, but she saw nothing amiss. Something watched them, but it stayed hidden beyond her craft.

George rode easily ahead of her, one with his mare, but Dinah could see the tenseness in his shoulders. He felt it too.

The girls had relaxed enough that they'd been chattering with excitement about their ponies. The geldings, good horses that they were, just flicked their dark ears and moseyed along.

They were now quiet and still, little hands tight upon their leather reins. Smart little rabbits.

The sun was kissing the hills as they rode up to the Blackham homestead. Mary's mama was waiting for her, standing on the front porch, arms crossed tightly against her chest. Maybe she did care.

"Get on over here, girl."

Maybe not.

Mary dismounted and ran inside. Her mama followed.

George tied a lead rope to the riderless pony's bridle through the bit rings and attached it to a ring on Lolly's saddle.

"You're going to be in charge of both your pony and Buck, here," he said to Lolly. "You can do that, right?"

Lolly nodded, green eyes wide.

The three of them and their steeds, and Buck by himself, continued to the Pickton ranch. The sun was close to setting and it was getting cold fast. Dinah tasted ice on the western wind that whipped up as the last of the sunlight haloed the hills.

A cloud of grasshoppers tornadoed out of the grass in front of Lolly, and her pony shied. Lolly screeched and hung on to the saddle horn as he full on bolted, dragging poor Buck along with him.

The grasshoppers coalesced into one giant grasshopper, its deep black eyes flaring hungrily in the last red gleam of the sun. It hopped after the ponies and Lolly, muscular legs propelling it ten yards for each hop. It chattered as it leaped, clacking and hissing.

The ponies had no chance.

The giant beast reached up with one spiny foreleg, then slammed it through Buck's spine, pinning the pony to the dirt. Buck screamed piteously, the sound shattering Dinah's heart.

Lolly's pony was yanked back. Dinah could see Lolly's tear streaked face as she tried to detach the lead rope, then gave up and dismounted, running further away from the grasshopper— and Dinah and George.

Dinah adored her mule Malyu. But Malyu's strengths were in bravery and persistence, not speed. George kicked his mare past the both of them, drawing and aiming his rifle as he galloped past.

He fired twice, the crack splintering through the chittering of the creature. Dinah could see, *See-Clearly*, the bullet hit Buck's head, killing him instantly.

The other bullet hit the grasshopper. Dinah knew it did. It was like hitting a barn door. If George could get off that desperate trick shot of hitting Buck's skull, there was no way he could miss the grasshopper. But the monster shimmered into the horde of tiny insects as the bullet passed through.

That also allowed it to free its leg from Buck.

And to hop after Lolly, solidifying again into a single monstrous beast.

Though *hop* sounded so bland for something so terrifying.

One lunge took it past Lolly's pony.

The second halved the distance to Lolly.

And the third brought it right atop of her.

George urged Dipper towards the creature, past poor Buck. His Appaloosa mare was the night sky on four hooves, tearing towards it like the icy wind out of the North.

Dinah tucked down and coaxed Malyu, fast as she could go, but by the time she too reached Buck's body, she knew she had no chance of catching the creature. She rose up in the stirrups, holding the thunderbird feather in front of her, willing her *See-Clearly* amulet to grant her night sight as well as cutting through illusions.

Just one clear shot, just one, and she could loose the lightnings and burn that creature back to the hell it had come from....

But it was too close to Lolly. Too close to risk the lightnings, even with *Strike-True*. She'd used that for shooting, and stabbing, but not releasing the lightnings.

She could see the muzzle flare as George fired, but no bullet damaged the shimmering creature.

It morphed once more, into the old Native man she'd seen at the saloon. He grabbed Lolly and stuffed the screaming girl into his woven basket. It expanded to contain her writhing body.

Then he disappeared.

~

"I CAN'T WAIT a month til he attacks again. Maybe Lolly's still alive." Dinah drained the glass of whiskey George had bought for her, rubbing the smudged glassware with her thumb. The top of the glass was nicked, and it cut her thumb. Her blood ran in thin rivulets inside the glass to mix with the dregs of whiskey.

George motioned, and Mr Augustin, the saloon owner and barkeep, brought over the rest of the bottle. George refilled Dinah's glass, and topped off his own and Miss Bordelon's, who sat across from Dinah.

"Haakapainiži," Miss Bordelon muttered. "I thought I was just telling tales to keep the children alert."

Dinah didn't comment. Both she and George had closely studied the spot from which he'd taken Lolly. Dinah had collected a handful of dead grasshoppers, but there was no other sign. Her *See-Clearly* amulet was no help other than helping find the dried-up little insect bodies. George caught Lolly's pony, retrieved Buck's tack, muttering over the condition of the stabbed saddle, then they both rode slowly back to Boot Hill. Lolly's pony came up lame halfway home, and George's fretting over the surviving pony was too much for Dinah to bear. She'd ridden off ahead, to let Miss Bordelon know about Lolly.

Then they met up at the saloon. It was close to midnight, the Milky Way softly glowing in the icy sky. Inside the saloon it was warm with the crush of gamblers and drinkers.

Dinah swigged her glass of blood-tinged whiskey, then placed her hand over the top when George tried to fill it. "Coffee," she said. "I need coffee. I'm going back out to hunt down this creature."

"I'm going with you--"

"No, you aren't, George. This calls for magic, not bullets. We already tried the latter. I will ask to borrow your canniest, meanest, fastest horse, though."

She turned to Miss Bordelon. "Those kids, they all shared misery, right? You think that monster feeds off that as much as flesh?"

"Could be," Miss Bordelon said. "Back in Louisiana I'd heard of haints drawn to those suffering."

"Well, I can dredge up misery, right enough." She thought of her dead parents, how alone she'd been the last ten years, half Chinese, half white, not fitting in with the Chinese or whites.

How many times she thought she'd found companionship, only to be betrayed.

How many times she failed, trying to help innocents.

"I can feed him some misery."

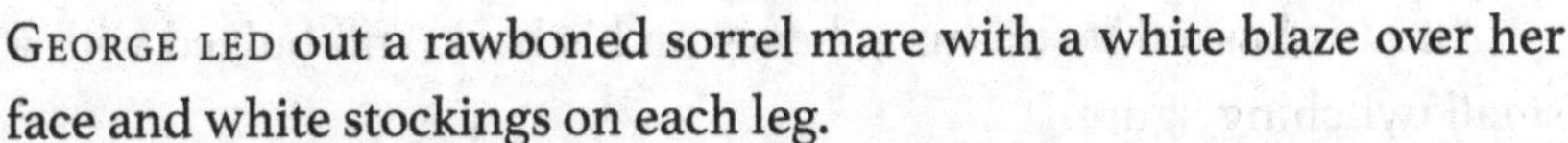

GEORGE LED out a rawboned sorrel mare with a white blaze over her face and white stockings on each leg.

"She'll go for you," he said, watching as Dinah blew in the mare's nostrils, offering her breath to tall watchful mare. "She's a fighter. Name's Red. Ask, don't demand, and she'll work out her heart for you."

The mare whuffed in Dinah's hair, lipping some of the stray strands. "She'll suit. Thank you, George." Dinah accepted a boost up into the saddle, then turned the mare down the street, back out towards the Blackham homestead.

The mare settled into a surprisingly comfortable trot. Dinah held the reins in one hand, the thunderbird feather in the other. She'd anointed her amulets with her blood. She was as ready as she could be.

Shooting stars flashed across the sky. Dinah wished upon them, each and every one, that she would find Lolly safe.

Then, gritting her teeth, she pictured finding Lolly's torn up body. Pictured the broken picked bones of the other children, flesh consumed by a horde of insects. Pictured Mary being taken, stabbed through like poor Buck.

Thought about her friend Jack Robertson, whose land was being poisoned. How she wasn't able to help him. Thought of the Jackrabbit Girl, whose heart she broke. Of Katy McGinnes' lovesick stableboy Danny, who died when Dinah was able to protect herself, but didn't think to protect him too.

Her parents. Her mama, a Chinese whore. Her papa, the white professor who fell in love with her and helped her get herself out of slavery. The both of them, who up and died of yellow fever back in the city of Washington D.C., when they were establishing Dinah as a viable candidate for colleges.

Her parents, who died because of her.

Oh, she was full of misery. A veritable feast.

Haakapainiži swarmed right in front of her, little insect bodies blurring into his old man form, stooped over two canes. His chitinous eyes gleamed with hunger.

And his basket! It still hung heavy on his back, still bulged with a small twitching figure.

Dinah crumpled the thunderbird feather in her hand, mashing down the spine, ignoring how it pricked her palm and drew blood.

"Take off your basket, Haakapainiži. I have a child for you, one far better than that mewling creature in your basket."

He clacked at her, the chittering of an insect, not the voice of a man, but removed his basket.

Dinah pressed so hard the feather, mixed with her blood, formed an irregular lump. She dismounted.

"Here it is," she said, walking towards Haakapainiži, holding out the mashed up thunderbird feather.

He half hopped, half shuffled to her, head cocked.

"Take it," she said.

One more shuffle hop, and he was only a few feet away. He lurched his head forward, his neck stretching like a snapping turtle, and yanked the feather from her and into his mouth...

...and stabbed one of his canes at her, right through her belly, as if he were stabbing poor Buck all over again.

She couldn't catch her breath to scream, it hurt so bad. She could feel warmth soak her shirt, then her wool coat, both the front and the back.

Focus. *Focus.* As she crumpled to the ground, tasting burnt copper in her mouth, she pulled on every moment of sorrow, of regret, and used that to link her blood pouring out onto the dry desert grass, with that blood soaking the feather resting in the creature's gullet.

And then, staring up at the shooting stars, she called the lightnings.

George and Miss Bordelon found Dinah before dawn the next morning.

Leastwise that's what Miss Bordelon told her two days later.

Lolly had clambered out of the woven basket and realized she herself couldn't do a thing for Dinah. Lolly sweet-talked the tall mare into laying in the grass, got astride, and rode hellbent for Boot Hill City.

She found George and Miss Bordelon, still in the saloon, awash with whiskey but sobering up quickly enough when they saw Lolly.

"And then she guided us back to you," Miss Bordelon said, wiping at Dinah's forehead with a damp cloth scented with tincture of rose. Sunlight streamed through the curtains of Dinah's boarding room bed chamber.

"We got you back here to the doctor," Miss Bordelon continued, her brown eyes rich with concern. "He said you were halfway healed already, else you'd be dead. We found this on you."

She held out a small pouch of gray felted material.

Dinah sat up, wincing. Half healed wasn't full healed.

She opened the pouch. Three turquoise stones tumbled out, along with a sprinkling of sage and willow. She sniffed the pouch. Despite the herbs, it smelled doggy, pungent and musky, with an overlay of sweet tobacco.

Coyote.

She stroked the pouch, and she could hear him. *"Laughin' at me splashing in a well, darlin'? You're damn lucky I got myself out. Else I'd not be around to save your skin."*

"Coyote," Dinah murmured, and thought she heard a yodeling yip.

"He's real, too?" asked Miss Bordelon. That voice like honey, the wonder in it stirring Dinah's heart.

"So much is real, you don't even know, Miss Bordelon." Dinah reached for her hand. "But I can teach you, if you'd like."

Dinah had friends here. Maybe, for once, she would stay in one place for awhile.

Maybe she could make Boot Hill City home.

THE GRAND OPENING OF THE RESTAURANT AUGUSTIN

Dinah leaned back, crossing her booted feet at her ankles. She sat along the back wall in the corner of the Saloon Augustin where she could watch both the bar (busy) and the front door (shut against the evening chill). She sipped at her warm cider, burying her nose in the cup, enjoying the fruity cinnamon odor, almost covering the unwashed stink of the gamblers and cowboys filling the rest of the saloon.

Gods above and below, nothing could truly remove that odiferous miasma from one's nostrils. It was so bad she was sore tempted to deploy an amulet, any that might help the tiniest bit.

Dead of winter and no one had anything better to do but gamble and whore. But, apparently, not bathe.

Her friend Caroline Bordelon slid into the chair across from her and rested her elbows on the stained pine tabletop, rounded chin cupped in her hands. *She* smelled fresh, tincture of rose.

"Evenin', Dinah," Caroline drawled in that honey thick accent of hers. She sure looked pretty in that new dress she'd sewn up, all lace-edged royal blue gingham that set off her oak brown skin.

She'd offered to make a dress for Dinah, but Dinah preferred to stick with her trousers and men's shirts and sturdy woolen vests.

Easier to get around. Life as a travelling sorceress was hard enough otherwise. Bad enough she had to deal with prejudice and hate, being the daughter of a white man and a Chinese prostitute. Dealing with skirts and petticoats and corsets? No, thank you.

Though she'd not been doing as much travelling recently. Somehow early winter had turned to mid, snow packed on the peaks and dusting the town streets, and she was still here in Boot Hill City.

Her friend George Kinman, the black owner of the town's largest livery stable, had strong armed the townspeople into donating what amounted to a large sum of cash, for her destroying a monster who'd settled in to steal and eat their children.

Enough, in fact, to keep her and her mule Malyu in comfort over the winter, and still have some left over for supplies and travelling expenses come spring. She'd been sore hurt, stabbed straight through the belly, and was just now able to ride a bit again, anyways.

"Mrs Augustin cookin' up something special for supper?" Caroline asked. The Augustins, a French couple who'd sought to make their home in the Deseret Territory, owned the saloon and the building next door.

Rumor had it that Mrs Augustin wanted to open up a restaurant in that empty building, and all the tasty dishes she cooked and sold at the saloon were just practice for when she did.

"Beef with red wine, roasted potatoes, carrots, and some other things growing in her garden," Dinah said. "They butchered Mr Jensen's old milk cow the other day."

"Doesn't matter how stringy the cow, Mrs Augustin works her culinary magic," Caroline said. "Back in New Orleans, she'd've prospered. Folks like good cookin' there."

Right then Mr Augustin placed two platefuls in front of them. "Enjoy, ladies," he said. "Let me know what you think."

Dinah leaned over her plate and inhaled. Rich chunks of braised beef, the tang of red wine, a zip of peppercorns. Creamy sautéed bitter greens dotted with flakes of dried red chilis. Roasted baby potatoes, their crispy golden jackets flecked with salt and thyme.

She took a hasty bite of beef before the bit of drool hanging off her lip could drip down her chin, then chewed slowly, letting the rich bloody juices fill her mouth. She then spooned up a taste of the greens, the interplay between the heat of the chilies and the fat of the cream dancing on her tongue. The crunch of the roasted potatoes, with the burst of warm creaminess once she bit down, set off the softness of the greens.

It was a symphony on a chipped porcelain plate.

"Let Mrs Augustin know she's outdone herself, Mr Augustin," Dinah said. "It's delicious."

"I'm pleased to hear it, Miss Dinah," Mr Augustin said, but he wasn't smiling. He was a round man with a neat beard and a sweeping, waxed mustache that was his pride and joy. His macassar oil, smoothing his hair back, smelled of bergamot and vanilla. He wore a stained cotton apron over trimly tailored trousers, a crisply pressed cotton shirt, and a black wool waistcoat lined with red embroidered silk.

"Might I speak with you after you've enjoyed your meal?" he said.

"Most certainly." Dinah watched him as he walked away, noting the tension in his back now she was paying attention. She was gettin' lazy and soft, just sitting around this winter, and not just in her body.

"Wonder what that's about," Caroline said between mouthfuls.

"I don't know," Dinah said. "But I'll let you know, soon as I find out."

TURNED out it wasn't Mr Augustin who wanted to talk to Dinah, it was Mrs Madeleine Augustin. Mr Augustin escorted Dinah to their building next door, where Mrs Augustin was working in flickering kerosene lantern light at a desk in the front room. Several clothbound, ink-blotched ledgers lay in front of Mrs Augustin, one opened with the page half full of small, neat writing.

Dinah, taking advantage of Mrs Augustin's concentration, surveyed the room. The flooring was waxed, smoothed, well-laid pine, no gaps to the space beneath. The faint aroma of sawdust and beeswax filled her nose.

The walls were paneled in white painted pine, with unlit gas sconces with blown glass shades at regular intervals. A few dining tables were already neatly arranged near the glass-paned front windows, with ladder-backed chairs tucked underneath. A door behind Mrs Augustin's desk led to what Dinah guessed would be the kitchen.

Mrs Augustin dabbed her fountain pen into a inkwell and scribbled one more note before acknowledging the two of them. Her light gray eyes were reddened. Stress, not grief, Dinah surmised.

"Thank you for coming over," Mrs Augustin said, her lilting voice reserved. She stood, unsteady, and nodded to Dinah, before drooping back into her chair.

Mr Augustin dragged a chair over from one of the tables and set it by the desk for Dinah. "I'm going back to the saloon, my dear," he said to his wife. "Thank you, Miss Dinah, for your time." He left.

Dinah had met Mrs Augustin only a few times prior. Mrs Augustin worked in the kitchen, and apparently kept the books, letting Mr Augustin be the face of their business at the saloon. Dinah wasn't quite sure how Mrs Augustin kept her trim figure, given the richness of the food she cooked. On second look—gaunt, not just trim. Mrs Augustin looked unwell.

"Sit, please," Mrs Augustin said.

Dinah did, stretching out her trouser-clad legs in front of her.

"I have need of your services, Miss Dinah. I fear someone doesn't want my restaurant to succeed. Though, Lord only knows, this town is in dire need of decent food," Mrs Augustin said. "I need you to find out who, or at least thwart them, until after opening night. The Restaurant Augustin *shall* be the talk of the territory, drawing gentlemen and women from as far away as Salt Lake City."

"Why do you think someone is out to ruin your restaurant?" Dinah asked.

Mrs Augustin gestured to the dining tables. "I had ten tables and groups of chairs on order. Six of the ten arrived broken to bits, their only use as kindling."

Dinah wasn't one to talk herself out of a job, but .... "That could just be an accident."

"All recent shipments of my supplies have had items missing or broken. *All* of them."

Accidents, theft, sheer bad luck. Dinah decided not to argue. "Give me access to this place and the saloon, assuming you keep supplies there as well. I'll set up some protective charms and see if I can trap anyone trying to hex you."

"My gas stove is arriving in Paradise City in two days via the Deseret Express and Union Pacific. From there I've hired Nathaniel Hummond to cart it down here. Can you accompany him?" Mrs Augustin leaned forward, thin hands grasping Dinah's. "I've put most of my money in that stove, Miss Dinah. It's to the be the cornerstone of my business. Amazing precision, the height of culinary science. It'll allow me to bring high cuisine to Deseret." For just a moment, her face shone like an angel's.

Dinah, who'd never cooked anything except in a pan over an open flame, nodded. "I understand its importance to you, Miss Augustin. I'll make sure it arrives safely."

~

DINAH ENDED up tossing her bedroll onto the floor of the restaurant that night rather than sleeping in her cozy room at Mrs Hale's boarding house.

She slept well. No one came by the restaurant. Dinah didn't know if it was her presence, or just that no one had any real designs on the place. Didn't matter. She had a job to do.

Dinah spent the morning crafting a handful of charms, enough for each window and doorway into the restaurant, and a few for the saloon as well. Bone and minerals, fur and feathers, bound together with a bit of kitchen grease from the small kitchen back of the saloon, with drops of Dinah's own blood to tie them to herself. *Watch-Close,*

Alarm, Mean-Well. She doubted the latter would deter anyone out to do harm, but it couldn't hurt to try.

After she'd made and placed the charms, she went to see George Kinman, snowflakes dappling her long black hair as she jogged down the street to his livery stable.

The main building for the livery stable, built of white-washed pine, with a central hard packed dirt corridor and stalls on either side, smelled like fresh hay and warm horseflesh. George kept it impeccably clean, hiring a couple children to muck out the stalls daily. It was cozy inside, despite the flurries of snow sticking to the roofs outside. Dinah had fashioned *Keep-Warm* charms for each stall. She had to re-invoke them weekly, but it was worth it to keep the creatures safe and comfortable.

"I'd like to borrow that sorrel mare of yours again," she said, leaning over a stall door, watching George groom his black appaloosa mare Dipper. "I have a feeling I might need a bit of speed. Malyu's built for the long steady haul." Malyu, her trusty mule, snorted from a stall down a ways upon hearing her name.

"Red Rose?" George said, straightening up, patting Dipper on her soft white nose. "She's available. Happy to let you use her, Dinah. Tomorrow morning?"

"Thank you, yes. First thing. I have to ride to Paradise. I doubt there will be any trouble, but I told Mrs Augustin that I would accompany Nathaniel Hummond and that stove of hers back from the train station. Shipped all the way from France." Dinah shook her head. "Can't rightly say I understand the need for a fancy bit of cooking equipment, but I do enjoy her cooking. And given that's part of how she's paying me, I'm not one to question her."

DINAH'S SUPPER that night was roasted pork loin with spiced apple compote and caramelized root vegetables. She swooned at the succulent pork, bursts of fat popping as she bit through the clove flavored crisp outer layer. The apple compote, just shy of tart enough to pucker her tongue, zinged in her mouth, accentuating the sweet pork. And she'd never liked root vegetables before, thinking they'd best stay buried in the ground, but she devoured every last bit of earthy sweetness, scraping her plate to get all the caramelized bits.

If Mrs Augustin could do all this with a simple hearth and wood fire, worn and tired as she looked, what magic could she perform with her newfangled stove?

That night, Dinah slept in her own bed at the boarding house, relying on the charms at the restaurant to alert her of anything untoward.

Toward morning, dawn just tinting the indigo sky with pink, a sense of dread wakened her. When she reached out to the *Alarm* charm, half asleep still, her arm hairs prickling, the dread faded. If someone meant harm, they changed their mind.

She got up. No point trying to go back to sleep. She dressed quickly and quietly. Heavy faded black canvas trousers, warm woolen socks Caroline had knitted for her, a blue cotton shirt, and her new thick wool coat, purchased for this winter.

Sunlight was just touching the tops of the mountain peaks as she walked around the restaurant before heading to the stable. A curious ginger cat, fur fluffed against the cold, watched her crouch down in the snow-dusted dirt to look under the raised porch, then climb up on the slick railing to look on top of the porch roof. Nothing. She caught a whiff of sour sweat and tobacco and the faintest touch of bergamot, but that could be nearly anyone in the town.

George was long up, taking care of the horses. He ladled out some thick brewed coffee for her when she entered the stable.

"Red's already packed up," he said. "I'll bring her round out front."

"Thank you, George." She drank the bitter coffee, wishing for a bit of honey.

She went to Malyu's stall, rubbing her soft mulish nose, giving her a small handful of sweet feed as a treat.

"Sorry, girl," she whispered to the mule, Malyu's long ears flicking forward. "Wisht I could bring you, but I have to travel a bit faster today."

She greeted Red Rose, the rawboned rangy sorrel mare, blowing softly in her nose, before accepting a leg up from George. The mare stood a good six inches taller at the withers than Malyu.

"Hummond drove up yesterday," George said. "Train, according to the schedule they posted last fall, should be getting in before you arrive. It's only ten miles or so, so I'll be looking out for you around sundown."

"Thanks, George. And don't fret. I'll take care of your gal, here," she said, patting the mare's fuzzy neck. She squeezed her legs and kicked Red Rose into the mare's smooth trot, her hooves dusting up bits of snow and dirt.

DINAH REACHED Paradise City as the train was departing just prior to noon. The town, twice as big as Boot Hill City, bustled. Folks dashing all about, the general store and other businesses kept busy. Dinah noted three restaurants in as many blocks, and three times as many saloons. A Native man, likely Navajo, aided by a pair of shaggy dogs, drove a small herd of Churro sheep down the main street towards some livestock pens, the stench of their wet wool overwhelming all the other smells.

Red Rose took it all in, her gait loose and easy. Dinah had kept her to a walk most of the ways. Her belly ached where she'd been run through, her muscles tight and quivering from the stress of riding.

The milky winter sunlight gleamed off the train engine as it chugged south to Jackalope Springs. She found Hummond at the back of the train station, cursing in three different languages at two men wrestling a large wooden crate into his cart, snapping a bull whip at their feet. His pair of mules twitched their ears at the commotion, but stood quietly, thin tails swishing at flies.

"That's the stove, I take it?" she said once it was all loaded up.

Hummond looked at her after paying the men, who scurried off before he could heap further abuse upon their poor heads.

"You're my nanny, I take it?" he said. He was short and swarthy and heavy set, with a thick graying beard covering most of his face. He reminded her of an old badger, nasty tempered and foul smelling.

Dinah didn't know if his mocking her was because she was a woman or Chinese. She didn't care. She had a job to do: get this short tempered idiot back to Boot Hill City with Mrs Augustin's stove. The latter needed to be in working condition; the former didn't.

"If that's what you're needin'," she replied. "The road is clear. Couple patches of deep snow about a mile up by the pass, but your mules should be fine."

He sneered. "I know what me and my mules can do."

She shrugged, then followed him out of Paradise, letting him lead with the precious stove.

❧

THEY WERE MORE than halfway back to Boot Hill City when the rear axle on Hummond's cart broke.

Dinah didn't know what was worse, the crack of the axle or the thunderous curses emanating from Hummond.

She didn't want to leave the wagon. More correctly, she didn't want to leave the stove.

"You'll need to ride either to Boot Hill or back to Paradise to get a new axle," she commented. "I'm staying here with the stove."

She dismounted, wincing, then traced her hands over the wheels and cart while Hummond blustered. Her fingertips prickled when she reached the rear wheels. She smelled bergamot and vanilla.

"You've been hexed," she said quietly, when he stopped shouting long enough to take a breath.

"I've *what*?!"

"Hexed, you idiot. Someone got to your cart and hexed the axle to break. Didn't you think to keep an eye on your cart?"

Fact was, Dinah should've checked the cart before he had left yesterday. She just hadn't thought about it, then. This was her fault, maybe more so than his. She hadn't taken Mrs Augustin seriously enough.

She moved on to the mules, whispering softly to them, checking their bodies, their feet. There. Vanilla. The front right shoe on one mule was loose, the hex on the iron causing her fingertips to tingle. The second mule itself was fine, but its harness was hexed. Bergamot. One leather strap would break before they got back to Boot Hill City.

"You have the faster horse," he said, ignoring her comment. "You ride back for aid."

She didn't have a choice. She doubted he had tack for the mules for riding, and the one mule with the loose shoe was likely to turn up lame. She dug in her pouch for amulets she could fix to the crate with the stove. *Touch-Not, Alarm, Do-No-Harm.* Best she could do, on short notice, gashing the meat of her thumb and anointing each with her own blood.

"Don't touch the crate with the stove. Don't look at it. Don't even think about it, or these will rebound on you." She urged Red past Hummond, the cart, and the mules, then rode for Boot Hill City.

ANOTHER MULE, new harnesses, a new axle, someone competent to repair the axle, and an entire additional rig including a driver and mules if Mrs Augustin wanted her stove before midnight. Dinah ran through the list in her head and couldn't come up with an easier way. The mule with the loose shoe needed to be walked back. She wouldn't trust that harness on the other mule until she could properly unhex it, never mind the cart itself.

She'd only ridden a mile down the trail, trying to ignore the scattering of snow flakes flurrying about as the sun dropped lower, when she heard an explosion.

"Gosh-darned gnat-brained idiot," she said, kicking Red into a canter back where she'd left Hummond.

Thank the seven gods he'd taken the mules out of their harness and tied them out where they could graze on some dried up grass her mare Red wouldn't even bother to piss on.

Because all that was left of the cart, the crate, the stove, and Hummond, was a smoldering pile of rubbish.

~

SEVERAL HOURS LATER FOUND DINAH, Red, and the two mules back at Kinmen's Livery.

George prepared a warm mash for all three of the equines and got one of his apprentices to work grooming them.

"The wagon's a complete loss," Dinah said. "One of yours?"

George shrugged. "Mules are fine. That's what matters."

He cleared his throat. "Dinah, did something go wrong with your amulets? To set the explosion off?"

"George, even if Hummond had opened the crate, despite my amulets, he'd've suffered no worse than a headache and blistered fingers. I truly don't know what happened. I'm thinking I missed a hex, maybe something on the stove itself. I don't know. It's all gone."

"Reason I'm asking, Dinah, is because the restaurant caught fire after you left this morning. It started all along the door frames and window frames. The building's half burned down. The Augustins managed to save some of the tables and chairs, but it'll take weeks to fix it all back up.

"Mr Augustin is saying it's your fault."

~

TIME WAS, Dinah would be packed up and already riding out of town. She'd done it before, on the heels of someone else's bad luck and loss, when she was the one likely, though unjustly, to take the blame. But she was tired and her belly muscles ached and damn it, she had friends here, and she'd done nothing wrong!

She wasn't running, not this time.

She marched right over to the Saloon Augustin, not even stopping at the burnt out husk of the restaurant next door. It was quiet, just a few gleams of light visible through between the door frame and the door.

As she slammed open the saloon door, ready to barge in, a wave of disgust and fear and guilt rolled over her, scented with bergamot and vanilla. *Go-Away* hex, in spades.

Someone had hexed the doorway. Hexed it against *her*.

She pushed through, ignoring the tingling in her palms. She was stronger, damn it. She strode to the bar, behind which Mr Augustin stood, polishing glassware with a damp cotton cloth.

Vanilla and bergamot.

"It was *you*," she spat.

"I don't know what you're talking about," Mr Augustin said, his eyes cold. "I believe the sheriff will be coming for you shortly, for destroying my property. And, I believe, for killing a man with witchcraft."

"I didn't do a darn thing except try to help your wife. Your property, her dream. Her dream you just couldn't stomach. I smelled you, your magic, this morning, I just didn't put it together then. Did you just figure it was better to make sure both the building and stove was destroyed? Is that why you didn't let it burn this morning?"

"This cockeyed dream of hers was killing her," he said. "I couldn't talk her out of it. No one cares about our food here. Simple food and copious amounts of whiskey to wash it down, that's all they want. She was wearing herself to a wisp of herself for foolishness.

"And no one will take your word over mine."

"*She* can speak for herself," a soft voice came from the upper level of the saloon. "Emile, does she speak the truth? When you weren't able to talk me out of the restaurant, you took it upon yourself to destroy my dream?"

She wafted down the stairs, dressed in a robe over a sleeping gown, looking more like a ghost of a woman than a living one. Her voice was cold as the grave, as was the look she turned upon her husband.

"My love, look at yourself," he entreated. "Worn away to nothing with worry and stress. The saloon is enough, is it not?"

"It'll have to be, now," Mrs Augustin said bitterly.

The town's sheriff, Jack Ransom, stuck his head in through the door. "Mr Augustin? Is the Celestial woman here?"

Dinah bristled. Two months ago she'd saved this town from an evil monster eating their children.

"She is," Mrs Augustin said. "But it's not how my husband told you."

A week later, Dinah, Caroline, and George were seated at a table in what used to be the Saloon Augustin. The pine tabletop was dressed with a smoothly ironed white linen cloth. Heavy silver cutlery sat on top of an equally pristine folded linen napkin. Crystal wine glasses were half full of a light red wine.

"It was all my mama's," Mrs Augustin said, setting down a small plate in front of each of them. "The linens, the cutlery, the porcelain. I'd saved it for this day. Thank god I'd kept it in a trunk in the house."

"Here's a small bit of something to whet your appetites."

On each plate, centered with a drizzle of cherry sauce encircling it, sat a small crust of toasted bread with a whipped gray paste on top of it. "Try it," Mrs Augustin urged.

Caroline picked it up, swiped it in the sauce, and plopped it in her mouth. She chewed tentatively, then with gusto. "Oh dear lord, Mrs Augustin, what in tarnation is that? I think my mouth has died and met an army of angels."

Dinah nibbled at hers, trying to make each little taste last an eternity. Sweet salty silkiness from the paste, tartness to counter the fat, and the crunch of the toast to set off the texture.

If the woman had any magical skill, as well as culinary skill, there'd be no way to stop her. Dinah could learn some new skills with charm craft by learning how to cook like Mrs Augustin.

George had already finished his morsel, sighing in pleasure.

"Fatted chicken liver pâté, blended with my own herbs," Mrs Augustin said proudly. "Just you ladies—and gentleman!—wait for the next course." She removed their plates and bustled away to check on the other tables, equally full of appreciative patrons.

"I think that's the liveliest I've ever seen that woman," commented Caroline.

Mr Augustin was languishing in the one cell of the town's jail, waiting til someone could decide what to do with him. He hadn't intended to actually kill someone, he argued. Dinah wasn't in a mood to be merciful, but it wasn't up to her. Hummond had no kin, and no friends, no one else to speak for him. The sheriff muttered that Mr Augustin had a wife who might one day forgive him, and he was otherwise a fine upstanding citizen.

Regardless, Mrs Augustin didn't even want to breathe the same air as her husband right now. She'd put all her energy into opening her restaurant, fires and missing equipment and the loss of her precious stove not stopping her.

Mrs Augustin decided to work with the space she had, and the Saloon Augustin was now the Restaurant Augustin, serving both dinner and supper.

Tonight was the grand opening, and Dinah was Mrs Augustin's guest of honor. The rest of the restaurant was full, with patrons begging to be let in, and told to come back another night.

"Indeed it is," Dinah agreed. "Running the restaurant agrees with her."

"Fulfilling her dream agrees with her, and you helped with that," George commented.

"I don't feel I did all that much," Dinah said quietly. Hummond was a nasty tempered idiot, but he hadn't deserved being blown toi smithereens.

"You came back and told the truth," Caroline said. "That was the bravest thing I've seen you do."

"Braver than facing a grasshopper monster?" Dinah asked, thinking back to the creature who'd stolen and eaten children, as well as stabbed her through the belly before she could kill it.

Caroline squeezed her hand. "You've never lacked for physical bravery, that I know."

George nodded in agreement.

"And here's the second course," Mrs Augustin said, placing a larger plate in front of each of them. "Smoked trout with a dill lemon sauce. Bon appétit! More to come!"

Indeed, there was more to come. Good friends. A warm room.

And a home.

ABOUT THE AUTHOR

Since graduating from West Point, Stephannie Tallent has served in the Army as a Military Intelligence officer during Desert Storm, gotten a Zoology then a veterinary degree, worked as a small animal veterinarian, and designed and published knitting patterns and books.

Throughout all that she's always wanted to be a writer, and she's put all her type A, soft-spoken, invisible middle-aged woman focus on that goal, writing everything from fantasy to science fiction, mysteries and romance.

www.stephannietallent.com

Sign up for my newsletter!
https://www.stephannietallent.com/subscribe/

ALSO BY STEPHANNIE TALLENT

Short Story Collections

Gates of Wonder

The Chronicles of Dinah Lee Wright Vol 1

The Chronicles of Dinah Lee Wright Vol 2

Gratitude of the Ocean: Jolene Tomberlin Series

The Serpent in the Shallows: Jolene Tomberlin Series

The Monkey's Journal

The Kaleidoscope Jaguars of the Jungles of Mexicatl

The Mermaid of Ellis Prime

One Plus One Equals More (mystery/crime)

A Snowman Made of Sand (romance)